Who cares about
disabled
people?

illustrated by **Pam Adams**

Child's Play (International) Ltd
Swindon   **Bologna**   **New York**
© M. Twinn 1989   ISBN 0-85953-361-1 (hard cover)   Printed in Singapore
This impression 1992   ISBN 0-85953-351-4 (soft cover)
Library of Congress Catalogue Number 90-45704

Many people are handicapped.

Some are blind . . .

. . . or deaf

. . . or mute

They may have
something
wrong with
their brain,

. . . or be unable to use some of their limbs.

We can learn what it is like

to be handicapped.

Nearly everyone is handicapped in some way to a small extent.

To be very tall can be a help

. . . or a hindrance!

Even an exceptional talent can be a handicap.

We are all handicapped for a while if we are sick or injured.

We can handicap ourselves by drinking alcohol . . .

by taking drugs and smoking . . .

or eating too much, especially junk food.

These experiences should make us realise how fortunate we are most of the time.

Handicapped people have to put up with their disabilities all the time.

Many handicapped people can lead a normal life.

They work hard to develop talents
which help compensate for their disability.

Some have gifts which they share
with the rest of us.

Most handicapped people can do
many things for themselves.

Most
handicapped
people are
just like
you and me.

They can be kind and helpful . . .

But sometimes they may be thoughtless
and bad-tempered just like us.

Able bodied people should care for
handicapped people and help them . . .

. . . if they need or want help !

Handicapped people are often able to joke about their problem.

But we must never joke behind their back ! ! !

And it isn't nice to be stared at.
How do you like it ?

Handicapped people may need our help, but most of all
they need our time and interest. Never our pity !